IBEN SANDEMOSE

GRACIE & GRANDMA

UNDERWATER

Translation by
Tonje Vetleseter

MACKENZIE SMILES
San Francisco

WHEN GRANDMA PICKS UP GRACIE
FROM SCHOOL, GRACIE THINKS
THEY ARE GOING RIGHT HOME,
BUT THEY ARE NOT... GRANDMA
HAS SOMETHING IN THE CAR.

THE SWIMMING RING!
GRACIE KNOWS WHERE THEY
ARE GOING...TO THE
SWIMMING POOL!

"THE POOL IS FAR!" SHOUTS GRACIE.
"NOT IF WE COUNT UMBRELLAS
ALONG THE WAY," ANSWERS GRANDMA.
AFTER COUNTING 14 RED UMBRELLAS,
3 POLKA-DOT UMBRELLAS,
2 STRIPY ONES, AND
7 BLACK ONES, GRACIE
AND GRANDMA ARE
AT THE POOL IN
NO TIME AT ALL.

GRACIE AND GRANDMA PUT ON THEIR
SWIMMING SUITS IN A SMALL STALL.
"DONE," GRANDMA SMILES IN HER
NEW SWIMSUIT.
"BUT WE LEFT THE SWIMMING RING
IN THE CAR," REMEMBERS GRACIE.

"WE'LL BRING THE RING NEXT TIME,"
SAYS GRANDMA.

SO THEY GET DRESSED AGAIN, BUT
GRANDMA ONLY PUTS ON HER BOOTS
AND CARRIES AN UMBRELLA.
"CAN WE GO SWIMMING NOW?"
ASKS GRANDMA.
"NO," SAYS GRACIE.
GRACIE KNOWS SOMETHING
THEY HAVE TO DO FIRST.

SHOWER, OF COURSE! GRACIE CAN
JUST REACH THE SHOWER BUTTON.
SHE GETS A WARM SHOWER EVERY
TIME SHE PUSHES IT.
"AHHHHHH," SAYS GRACIE.
"THE CROCODILE IS WAITING,"
TEMPTS GRANDMA. BUT GRACIE
WANTS TO HAVE ONE MORE SHOWER,
AND ONE MORE, AND ONE MORE.

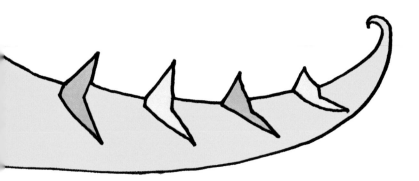

FINALLY, GRACIE SAYS "HI" TO THE
CROCODILE THAT GUARDS THE
POOL. GRACIE AND GRANDMA
PLAY SEAL AND STARFISH AND
SEA HORSE AND SHRIMP.

"I'M COLD," GRANDMA SHIVERS.
"LET'S WARM UP IN THE SAUNA."
BUT GRACIE CANNOT HEAR
GRANDMA BECAUSE GRACIE
IS NOW A DANGEROUS FISH
SWIMMING AT THE BOTTOM
OF THE SEA.

AFTER THEY SWIM, THE SAUNA IS WARM
AND FULL OF CLOUDS. GRANDMA PEEKS
IN AT GRACIE THROUGH THE GLASS DOOR.
"IT'S TIME TO COME OUT," SHE YELLS,
AND KNOCKS ON THE WINDOW.
"YOU ARE COMPLETELY PINK!"
"I WANT TO BE PINK," GRACIE
ANSWERS, AND STAYS
WHERE SHE IS.

NOW GRACIE WANTS TO SHOWER
AGAIN. SHE DARTS PAST GRANDMA.
AFTERWARD, THE HAIR DRYER
BLOWS GRACIE'S HAIR STRAIGHT
UP AND STRAIGHT OUT.

GRANDMA WRAPS GRACIE IN
A HUGE TOWEL.
"IT'S TIME TO GET DRESSED",
SAYS GRANDMA. NOBODY ANSWERS.
GRACIE IS GONE!

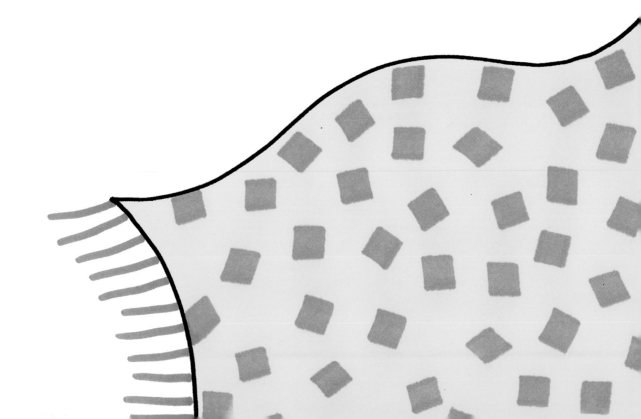

WHAT'S THAT SOUND?

GRACIE IS NOW A SMALL COW!
"MOO! ARE WE GOING HOME?"
ASKS THE SWEET, LITTLE COW.
BUT GRACIE AND GRANDMA ARE
NOT GOING YET.

BECAUSE FIRST THEY ARE GOING
TO EAT CHOCOLATE CAKE AND DRINK
APPLE JUICE.
"AND OLIVES," WHISPERS GRANDMA,
AND SHE TAKES A JAR OUT OF HER
POCKET. GRACIE SMILES. OLIVES
ARE WHAT GRACIE LOVES BEST!

Mackenzie Smiles, LLC
San Francisco, CA

www.mackenziesmiles.com

Originally published as
Fiat og Farmor Under Vann
by
© J.W. Cappelens Forlag A.S. 2003
www.cappelendamm.no

Original artwork & design by Iben Sandemose
The artwork in this book was drawn with ink and marker.

Translation by Tonje Vetleseter

Art production by Bernard Prinz

ISBN 978-0-9790347-4-9

Printed in China

10 9 8 7 6 5 4 3 2 1

Distributed in the U.S. and Canada by:
Ingram Publisher Services
One Ingram Blvd.
P.O. Box 3006
La Vergne, TN 37086
(866) 400-5351